BOOK ANALYSIS

Written by Camilo Casallas Torres
Translated by Emma Hanna

Half of a Yellow Sun

BY CHIMAMANDA NGOZI ADICHIE

BrightSummaries.com

CHIMAMANDA NGOZI ADICHIE

NIGERIAN WRITER

- **Born in Enugu (Nigeria) in 1977.**
- **Literary awards:**
  - Orange Broadband Prize for Fiction, 2007 (for *Half of a Yellow Sun*)
  - National Book Critics Circle Award for Fiction, 2013 (for *Americanah*)
  - MacArthur Genius Grant, 2008
- **Notable honours:**
  - Member of the American Academy of Arts and Sciences (elected in 2017)
- **Notable works:**
  - *Purple Hibiscus* (2003), novel
  - *The Thing Around Your Neck* (2009), short story collection
  - *Americanah* (2013), novel
  - *We Should All Be Feminists* (2014), essay

Chimamanda Ngozi Adichie grew up in the world of academia, as both of her parents worked at the University of Nigeria in Nsukka: her mother was the head of admissions, while her father was a professor of statistics. This is reflected in her work, as a significant proportion of *Half of a Yellow Sun* is set in the university. Furthermore, during the early years of her childhood she lived in a house that had previously been the residence of Chinua Achebe (1930-2013), who is generally considered the most influential Nigerian writer of the modern era – an incredible coincidence which seems to foreshadow her own literary career.

Adichie moved to the United States for university, and initially studied communications and political science at Drexel University in Philadelphia and Eastern Connecticut State University, before completing a Master's degree in creative writing at John Hopkins University in Baltimore in 2003. That year, she also published her debut novel *Purple Hibiscus*, a coming-of-age story which centres on a dysfunctional Nigerian family.

Since the publication of her first novel, Adichie has continued to write and publish fiction and non-fiction alike, and has received a number of awards in recognition of the way her writing has redefined English-language Nigerian and African fiction. She also obtained a second Master's degree in African studies from Yale University in 2008.

It is important to take this academic background into consideration when analysing the work of modern writers such as Adichie. Although society has traditionally had a tendency to assume that most authors are dashing adventurers like Lord Byron, whose madcap escapades are often even stranger than the stories they write, Adichie is part of a new generation of writers whose craft often draws more heavily on meticulous research and critical and literary theory than personal experience.

HALF OF A YELLOW SUN

THE BIRTH OF A NEW NATION

- **Genre:** novel
- **Reference edition:** Ngozi Adichie, C. (2007) *Half of a Yellow Sun*. London: Harper Perennial.
- **1st edition:** 2006
- **Themes:** colonialism, nationhood, race, war, language

Half of a Yellow Sun is a masterful, uncompromisingly brutal examination of the Nigerian Civil War, also known as the Biafran War. It tells the story of the twin sisters Olanna and Kainene, whose family is part of the Nigerian upper class, where corruption is rampant and often works in the favour of the British colonisers from whom the country has just won its independence instead of the people of Nigeria itself. The novel also focuses on Olanna's partner Odenigbo, a professor of mathematics with socialist leanings, and Richard, an aspiring British writer with whom Kainene falls in love.

The sisters' lives are thrown into turmoil when the country's tenuous hold on peace is threatened by the Hausa, a Muslim ethnic group, who seize control of the country and massacre the Igbo, the minority group that Olanna and Kainene belong to. This breathtaking novel navigates the themes of exile, mistreatment, death and betrayal to create an in-depth portrait of the era it is set in, and explores the thin line that separates hope and hate.

SUMMARY

ARRIVAL IN NIGERIA

The opening pages of the novel introduce the character of Ugwu, a young man from a humble background who has just moved to Nsukka to work as a houseboy for Odenigbo, who hosts intellectual debates and worries a great deal about the political and social stability of Nigeria. The pair soon develop a close bond.

However, Ugwu's peaceful life is disrupted when Odenigbo's girlfriend Olanna moves in with them. Olanna quickly takes charge of the house and the couple frequently engage in loud sex, but over time, Olanna and Ugwu also develop a close bond. All three are Igbo, but while Olanna and Odenigbo have both received an education, Olanna had a much more privileged upbringing than Odenigbo. Olanna goes against her father's wishes and begins working as a professor of sociology in Nsukka, and also breaks up with her rich Hausa ex-boyfriend, Mohammed, once and for all.

The reader soon learns that Olanna has a twin sister called Kainene, who is much more pragmatic and works for one of their father's companies. Kainene meets a British journalist and aspiring writer called Richard, who is dating a woman called Susan, and they fall in love. Kainene moves to Port Harcourt to manage the family business, while Richard moves to Nsukka to study traditional Igbo art and develops a fascination with the local culture there. He also becomes a member of Odenigbo's social circle, and starts attending their gatherings. Meanwhile, Ugwu starts attending primary school, and grows closer to Olanna and Odenigbo as his education progresses. However, the household's happiness is marred by the fact that Olanna's desire to have a child is never fulfilled.

DOMESTIC STRIFE

Olanna does not get along with Odenigbo's mother, who wishes that her son had chosen to start a relationship with someone else. After a fight between the couple, the distrust that Odenigbo's mother feels towards Olanna reaches fever pitch and, according to Ugwu, she performs some kind of witchcraft and forces Odenigbo to sleep with a servant girl called Amala.

Amala falls pregnant, and Olanna learns of the affair. Her relationship with Odenigbo begins to deteriorate, and she grows closer to Richard, with whom she eventually has sex. Afterwards, she tells Odenigbo everything, and he bars Richard from their house in a humiliated rage. Kainene also learns of the affair and is furious with her sister.

Amala gives birth to a baby girl, but does not want to take responsibility for the child. Olanna then decides to adopt the infant, feeling certain that this is the daughter she has always wanted. However, she is unable to decide on a name, and simply calls her Baby.

DEATH COMES KNOCKING

After a number of years go by, peace is restored in Olanna and Odenigbo's household, although Olanna and Kainene are not on speaking terms and Richard is not welcome there. Meanwhile, a group of Igbo dissidents launch a coup d'état against the ruling Hausa elite and assassinate a number of politicians. Olanna is one of the few characters who is left feeling uneasy in the wake of the coup, which is celebrated by her relatives.

Did you know?

Nigeria is a highly culturally diverse country, as it is inhabited by a variety of ethnic groups, and relations between these different groups are often strained. *Half of a Yellow Sun* discusses how the Hausa people received preferential treatment during the period when the country was colonised by the British, as they were perceived as more "civilised" than other ethnic groups because they were Muslim. This gave rise to a social structure in which the Hausa people became part of the establishment, collecting taxes and subjugating other ethnic groups, such as the Igbo and the Yoruba, in exchange for a tacit understanding that Christian missionaries would focus their attention elsewhere.

This social structure created tremendous inequality between the country's various ethnic groups and the geographical regions they hailed from: while northern Nigeria, which was chiefly inhabited by the Hausa, became increasingly rich and powerful, the south-eastern areas of the country were left vulnerable to exploitation at the hands of the British colonisers who only cared about their own economic interests.

The celebrations are short-lived, as the Hausa quickly form an alliance with the Yoruba and strike back at the Igbo, staging a second coup to seize back power and massacring the Igbo population. The situation spirals completely out of control, and train stations are filled with the injured. Seeing the chaos unfold, Olanna fears for her aunt and uncle's safety, and manages to make the perilous journey to the neighbourhood they live in with Mohammed's help. She discovers that they were killed by their own neighbours, and is shaken to her core. On the train back to the city, she encounters a woman who shows her a horrific sight:

> "Olanna looked into the bowl. She saw the little girl's head with the ashy-grey skin and the plaited hair and rolled-back eyes and open mouth. She stared at it for a while before she looked away. Somebody screamed." (p. 149)

The Igbo people attempt to secede from the rest of Nigeria and found a new country called the Republic of Biafra. Odenigbo approves of this development, as he believes that secession could benefit the country and put a stop to the massacres; however, it is already too late, and vast quantities of blood have already been spilled.

| Flag of the Republic of Biafra.

REPERCUSSIONS

Following the death of her aunt and uncle, Olanna is left unable to move her legs and feels utterly helpless, and Odenigbo's usually robust constitution is left weakened. Olanna and Richard are reunited when they both attend a conference about the war, which ends in a street protest led by Odumegwu Ojukwu (1933-2011), the leader of the Republic of Biafra. This sight captures the imaginations of both Olanna and Richard, who see him as a symbol of rebirth and renewal.

The family are in the middle of making preparations to attend Ugwu's sister's wedding when they are interrupted by the arrival of Nigerian military forces nearby and are forced to flee to Odenigbo's mother's house in Aba, where Odenigbo takes a job as a social worker. However, their newfound peace does not last long, as the town soon comes under attack from Hausa forces. The family are forced to flee once more, but Odenigbo's mother decides to remain in her hometown. This time, Olanna and Odenigbo end up in Umuahia, where Olanna begins working as a teacher and the couple get married; however, the wedding ceremony is interrupted by an air strike.

TRYING TIMES

Although their new life is far from stable and this terrifies Olanna, she tries to put on a brave face. When the school she works at is turned into a refugee centre, she decides to keep teaching in her home, with Ugwu's help. Meanwhile, Odenigbo learns that his mother has been killed. In his despair, he attempts to travel back to her hometown, determined to give her a proper funeral, even though he knows that the road will be full of Nigerian soldiers.

Elsewhere, Richard has been tasked with writing articles about the Biafra situation. He becomes quite well known for his work, which blends accurate coverage of the war with commentary on the untenable political situation and the hope that the war will soon come to an end, now that Nigeria is receiving aid from a number of foreign powers to fight against Biafra.

Odenigbo falls into a deep depression, and the family is forced to move into a tiny apartment. Ugwu is also approached by members of the Biafran army who are hoping to conscript him into their ranks on a number of occasions. The only spark of light in what seems to be a hopeless situation is a visit from Kainene, during which the sisters finally seem to put aside their differences. In the end, Ugwu succumbs to pressure from his peers and is conscripted into the army; he becomes a skilled fighter, and is held in high esteem by his comrades. However, this leads to his darkest moment when the other soldiers manage to talk him into raping a woman, leaving him haunted by the memory of the hate that burned in her eyes.

Shortly afterwards, Kainene informs Olanna that Ugwu has been killed in battle. The city comes under attack once again, and the family is forced to move in with Kainene and Richard. The twins grow closer and become inseparable once again, and everything seems to be looking up when they learn that Ugwu is actually alive. However, one day Kainene leaves to attempt to trade across enemy lines and disappears.

Ojukwu surrenders and the Republic of Biafra is dissolved. The family is able to return to Nsukka, but Kainene is still missing, and Richard throws all of his energy into searching for her.

A few years later, Ugwu returns to his hometown, where he discovers that his mother has died and his sister was raped. He starts writing a book about the war, and titles it *Narrative of the Life of a Country*. On the other hand, Richard has stopped writing, and Kainene is never seen again.

CHARACTER STUDY

The strength of *Half of a Yellow Sun* lies in its characters, who both drive the story forwards and frequently find themselves in opposition to it. Even as their lives are thrown into chaos by the events of the story, they find the strength of will to play an active role in the situations they find themselves in, creating richly layered characterisation. As Adichie says herself in the acknowledgements at the end of the book, some of the characters are based on real people, even if their stories have been fictionalised.

OLANNA

Olanna is a warm-hearted character who seems to act as a source of love and strength for everyone around her throughout the novel. According to her sister, her name means "God's Gold" (p. 58), and she is described as extremely beautiful. She also has a rebellious streak, and does not hesitate to confront her parents or her husband when she believes that they are becoming overly miserly, greedy or complacent.

However, she is also beset by sorrow throughout the novel, and often comes into contact with death. In fact, we have more insight into her personality than any of the other characters in the novel, as we get a first-hand perspective of her doubts and are provided with a detailed account of all the events that most deeply disturb her:

> "She described the vaguely familiar clothes on the headless bodies in the yard, the still-twitchy fingers on Uncle Mbaezi's hand, the rolled-back eyes of the child's head in the calabash and the odd skin tone – a flat, sallow grey, like a poorly wiped blackboard – of all the corpses that lay in the yard." (p. 156)

Although all the characters in the novel could justifiably be described as victims, Olanna arguably fits that description more than anyone else. She suffers a great deal over the course of the novel, and her tremendous capacity for empathy means that not only does the civil war harm her directly, but she is also deeply affected by the pain of those around her.

KAINENE

Even the meaning of Kainene's name ("Let's watch and see what next God will bring," p. 58) sets her apart from her twin sister. By nature, she is much more practical and forthright than Olanna, which leads her to take on significant responsibilities in her father's often shady business dealings. However, her personality also has hidden layers, and since we are never offered her perspective on the events of the story, or told how she feels about the other characters, her transformation over the course of the novel is much more subtle than her sister's. Richard initially describes her as witty, sly and "almost androgynous" (p. 60), but she eventually becomes much more open and even starts working with migrants. Furthermore, her disappearance is the defining moment of the closing section of the book, and acts as the final nail in the coffin of the hopeful world that the other characters once lived in, and must now learn to live without.

UGWU

Odenigbo frequently describes Ugwu as "ignorant", which is not an entirely inaccurate assessment: he grew up in a rural area where he did not have the opportunity to receive an education, and is therefore unaware of a great deal of political and social information that Olanna and Odenigbo have access to. However, he has a keen mind and, as the other characters frequently remark, he learns quickly. This combination of character traits is important, as it provides readers who may be ignorant of the political and cultural situation in Nigeria with a more realistic, nuanced understanding of the country and its people. In fact, the reader ultimately becomes familiar with the political conflicts that ravaged the country in the late 1960s through Ugwu's friendly, relaxed narrative voice, and at the end of the novel he begins writing his own comprehensive book about the war. In this way, he becomes the voice of an entire generation.

ODENIGBO

Odenigbo is a striking character with tremendous physical and mental capacities who embodies the concept of strength. He radiates energy and power everywhere he goes, but he also takes care of the people he loves. However, he differs from Olanna in that he does not have a limitless source of inner strength to draw on, and this strength can fail him at any moment. In this way, he bears a certain similarity to the hope that characterised the creation of Biafra, which is unstable, tempestuous and undefinable.

RICHARD

Richard is a shy man with a melancholic, introspective temperament. He is never particularly outspoken at meetings, and avoids risks until he meets Kainene. Through his relationship with her, he eventually becomes part of her family. His greatest ambition is to write about Nigeria and its art.

Although Richard initially observes the war from an external standpoint, he and his newfound family are by no means exempt from the suffering it wreaks, and he comes to consider himself Biafran. Adichie puts great care and consideration into the construction of his character, which adds a great deal of nuance to the novel as a whole. Although the novel is an overtly anti-colonialist work, and discusses the negative impact that British colonialism had on Nigeria at length, the character of Richard allows the complexity of these issues to be explored in greater depth, as his mentality shifts over the course of the novel until it more closely aligns with the ideals espoused by the African socialists than his European origins. However, Richard is not perfect by any means, and some of his comments can be condescending and racist. In other words, his character is a reflection of post-colonial Europe and its efforts to become more compassionate and human, and all the contradictions that accompanied this attempted transformation.

BABY

Baby does not play a particularly large role in the novel; she does not speak often, and appears in fewer scenes than the other characters. However, she is an intriguing character, who seems like a normal child at certain moments and a wise old woman trapped in a child's body at others. In fact, her hair begins falling out at one point, and Kainene tells Olanna that this is a sign of great wisdom. She plays with other children from every social class, and entertains herself by playing with a dagger that belongs to a soldier who was injured in combat. She is an unusual individual who is blessed with an utterly carefree attitude, knows exactly what to say in any situation, and spreads hope and happiness to everyone around her.

ANALYSIS

FORM

Multiple perspectives

Half of a Yellow Sun is a relatively long novel, and the plot unfolds at a relentless pace, frequently leaving the reader stunned by its thoughtful analysis of life in Nigeria. The novel is narrated in the third person, and the narrator is a nameless, omniscient figure who is able to see into the characters' thoughts and even seems to know what will happen in the future. This narrator is also emotionally detached, and even describes the genocide of the Igbo people, which was characterised by killings, persecution, disruption and the loss of all hope, with apparent indifference.

The identity of this voice is never made clear to the reader: it could be the voice of God, dispassionately observing the misfortune of the people on earth, or perhaps the voice of the author herself, writing about the events of the past from an analytical perspective that affords her greater emotional distance from the war than the people who lived through it. In any case, the function of this detached narrative style is to offer the reader a clear, seemingly impartial account of the ravages of this war, though the sheer brutality of the events depicted is likely to leave the reader emotionally exhausted by the time they turn the final page.

Although the narrator seems to be able to enter the characters' minds at will, the novel only features the perspectives of three characters: Ugwu, Olanna and Richard. Each chapter of the novel is told from the point of view of one of these characters (for example, the first chapter depicts Ugwu arriving at Odenigbo's house for the first time, where he takes a keen interest in the professor's belongings). Even though their perspectives are filtered through the lens of the omniscient third-person narrator, their voices are very clearly defined, and they each offer their own perspective on life in Nigeria. Ugwu's voice is defined by his humble background and ignorance, and his chapters allow the reader to understand the country's political situation as it was seen by the lower classes; Olanna offers a woman's perspective, and her chapters depict the devastating effects of gender-based violence while also focusing on themes such as motherhood and family; and finally, Richard offers an outsider's perspective, and discovers the realities of life in Nigeria, war and hopelessness in tandem with the reader.

Time

The novel is set in two distinct time periods, and alternates between them. Two sections of the novel depict the events of the early 1960s, while the other two sections are set in the later years of that decade. In both sections set during the early 1960s, the narrative is more heavily focused on the characters' life as a family. These chapters are dominated by the themes of jealousy, betrayal, love and parenthood, and depict the way the relationships between the characters disintegrate and are rebuilt over time.

Conversely, the two large sections which are set at the end of the decade are much more politically oriented. The characters are constantly forced to move from one place to another, and are frequently confronted with death as the fledgling Republic of Biafra struggles to find a foothold in the world.

These four sections alternate between the two different time periods, starting with a chapter set during the early 1960s. The perspective then switches to the end of the decade, and the other two sections follow the same pattern. In this way, information is parcelled out to the reader fairly gradually, with some pieces of information, such as the ways various characters had betrayed the other members of the family in the past, being alluded to in the second section, but never explicitly stated or explained until the full story is revealed in the third section.

One of the most interesting narrative devices employed by Adichie is to scatter short descriptions of the book that Richard wants to write, *The World Was Silent When We Died*, throughout the text. These short passages often give the impression that an external observer is reading Richard's work: "He argues that Nigeria did not have an economy until Independence. The colonial state was authoritarian, a benignly brutal dictatorship" (p. 204). Curiously, they seem to appear almost at random, without following any particular pattern.

However, these sections play an important role in enriching the reader's understanding of the novel's context. They do not just provide us with insight into the way Richard writes, but also offer us important information about the factors that caused the war, such as colonialism, religion and the conflicts between the various ethnic groups that coexist in Nigeria and the colonial forces. In a way, these sections play a similar role to the novel's shifting focus: in the same way that the novel jumps between different time periods in order to help the reader to understand the various stages of the Nigerian Civil War, the sections which focus on Richard's book help us to understand the earlier conflicts which shaped the country's past and present; for example, it explains why a significant proportion of the Igbo people live in poverty and why the British colonisers were more inclined to trust the Muslim Hausa. Furthermore, this shows us that the past was also characterised by death and inequality, and by exploring these tragedies from an anthropological, sociological and historical standpoint, the reader is left better equipped to comprehend and analyse the story told throughout the rest of the novel.

THEMES

Colonialism

Half of a Yellow Sun is an exploration of the causes of inequality and conflict in Nigeria, and its perceptive analysis of the relations between the British Empire and its colonies seems to suggest that colonialism was the root cause of these conflicts.

However, Adichie does not simply focus on the relationship between the coloniser and the colonised, emphasising the way that Britain and other European countries despoiled the nations of Africa during the colonial era; instead, she paints a detailed, nuanced picture of the complex political structures in Nigeria which often pitted one indigenous ethnic group or tribe against another, creating weaknesses that the colonial occupiers were quick to exploit. This allows the novel to paint a comprehensive portrait of this tangled web of power dynamics between the various social groups living in Nigeria.

For example, in addition to showing how the members of the lower classes of Nigerian society were affected by colonialism through Ugwu's perspective, the novel also explores the effects of colonialism on the lives of the members of the Nigerian upper classes, left-wing academics and religious orders. This approach allows Adichie to create a sprawling mosaic of diverse social relations instead of simply relying on a dichotomy of the oppressors versus the oppressed. Indeed, as we have already seen in the character study, the inclusion of the character of Richard allows for a more nuanced depiction of the British than a generalised portrayal of them as ruthless imperial overlords. In other words, every aspect of this complex novel contributes to our understanding of the story as a whole.

Nationhood and race

The title of the novel, *Half of a Yellow Sun*, is a reference to the flag of the Republic of Biafra, and echoes the themes that the entire novel is built on: namely, the hope that can fuel the birth of a new nation, and the ideals associated with this process.

The creation of Biafra raises a number of questions for the novel's characters and readers alike to think about: could Biafra represent a solution to the problems facing Nigeria? What defines a nation, and how should its borders be drawn? (After all, borders are not set in stone; today the border between Mexico and the US lies along the Rio Grande, but that border used to be further north.) And does a newly founded country gain its legitimacy through a simple proclamation of independence by its own citizens, or does this legitimacy depend on the international community's recognition of its status as a nation?

One particular question is constantly on Odenigbo's mind, and is one of the central concerns of the novel: will secession be beneficial for the Igbo and the Hausa? This is a fundamental ethical question, and Odenigbo initially believes that the ideal outcome would be for these different ethnic groups to live together in unity and peace. However, he gradually comes to believe that distributing the land between the two groups is a better way of restoring peace.

Richard has a different question on his mind: even though he is English, if he is present at the founding of the nation of Biafra, can he be considered a citizen of the country? These questions serve to illustrate the novel's fundamental message about nationhood: namely, that nations and borders are illusions. There is no nation that has existed since the dawn of time; as such, they must be human constructs. If that is the case, what does it really mean to be Nigerian, British, Spanish or Chinese? For example, the division between Biafra and Nigeria is based on ethnicity, as it was presumed that the Igbo people would live in Biafra and the Hausa would live in Nigeria. However, the novel is populated by a wide range of characters who cannot be neatly categorised into either of these groups: Mohammed is Hausa, but he helps the Igbo on several occasions; one of Odenigbo's closest friends is Yoruba, and worries about the family when she learns about the massacre; and Richard is English, but he considers himself Biafran and takes up the Biafran cause (although he later reconsiders his identity after a confrontation with Kainene).

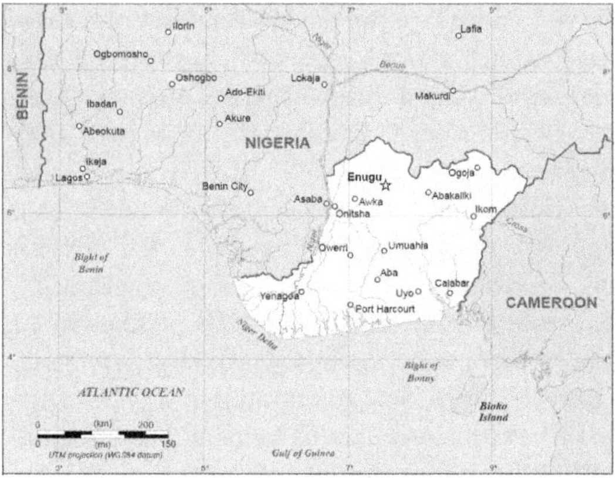

| Map of the border between Nigeria and Biafra.

The novel also explores the connection between nationhood and race as it applies to Nigerian history through frequent discussions of the theory that colonialism led to the Hausa and the Igbo being more strictly differentiated, as the two groups had never clashed on a major scale in the entire history of Nigeria prior to the colonial era, and it is said that the British had encouraged an arbitrary racial distinction between the two groups by affirming that the Hausa had lighter skin than the Igbo.

This leads to further questions: what really separates one social group from another? Are these divisions really based on race, nationality and religion, or are they more closely linked to the distribution of land and resources? Adichie frequently makes it clear that she leans towards the second of these views, and maintains that the conflict in Nigeria was largely motivated by economic and political factors such as power and inequality, rather than racial or ethnic factors.

War

In *Half of a Yellow Sun*, the scars of war and violence are most visible on the human bodies within the text. Some notable examples of this theme include decapitated heads, bodies which continue to twitch even after the life has bled out of them, rape, and wounds which, according to Olanna, look like lips on the verge of speaking. This is a key idea, as the mutilated bodies of the dead act as a message to the living. The paranoia that plagues Olanna is born in the moment she sees her aunt and uncle's dead bodies, as their corpses seem to be giving her a warning for the future: if it can happen to us, it could just as easily happen to you, your husband or your daughter.

Language

The theme of language intersects with the other ideas we have already examined, such as war and race. Corpses may communicate wordlessly with the living, but language is still the primary vehicle for communication, particularly to denote race, ethnicity or religion. For example, Richard witnesses one episode at the airport in which the Igbo are identified by what they can and cannot say:

> "'You are Igbo,' the second soldier said to Nnaemeka.
> 'No, I come from Katsina! Katsina!'
> The soldier walked over to him.
> 'Say Allahu Akbar!'
> [...]
> Nnaemeka knelt down. Richard saw fear etched so deeply onto his face that it collapsed his cheeks [...] He would not say Allahu Akbar because his accent would give him away. [...] the rifle went off and Nnaemeka's chest blew open, a splattering red mass." (pp. 152-153)

Similar scenes take place throughout the novel, allowing the theme of language to be explored. Certain sounds, idioms and words are associated with particular contexts, and language is linked to a person's cultural and geographic origins, meaning that the use of specific language can be used to engender violence or inspire hope. There is even a strange instance of onomatopoeia, when the bleating of a goat provides great amusement for Olanna's family because the sound resembles a song, and is also similar to the sound that the Hausa leader allegedly made when his throat was slit.

FURTHER REFLECTION

SOME QUESTIONS TO THINK ABOUT...

- What additional obstacles do you think women face when trying to write, publish and sell novels, in comparison to their male counterparts? What additional barriers do you think a black author like Adichie would have to overcome?
- Why do you think Richard gave up trying to write his novel and decided to devote himself exclusively to journalism?
- What role do you think academics play in a country's political situation?
- Why do you think Adichie chose to w Olanna's perspective instead of Kainene's?
- Odenigbo frequently advocates the establishment of a socialist system of government in Biafra. Do you think he is right, or should they have adopted a different system of government?

We want to hear from you!
Leave a comment on your online library
and share your favourite books on social media!

FURTHER READING

REFERENCE EDITION

- Ngozi Adichie, C. (2007) *Half of a Yellow Sun*. London: Harper Perennial.

REFERENCE STUDIES

- Ekwe-Ekwe, H. (No date) *The Biafra War and the Age of Pestilence*. [Online]. [Accessed 19 April 2018]. Available from: <http://www.litencyc.com/theliterarymagazine/biafra.php>
- Jacobs, S. (2011) Orientalism in Sub-Saharan Africa. *Africa is a Country*. [Online]. [Accessed 19 April 2018]. Available from: <http://africasacountry.com/2011/04/orientalism-in-sub-saharan-africa>
- Martin, Á. (2017) Chimamanda Ngozi Adichie, la feminista transgresora. *El Espectador*. [Online]. [Accessed 19 April 2018]. Available from: <http://www.elespectador.com/noticias/cultura/chimamanda-ngozi-adichie-feminista-transgresora-articulo-674988>
- Sandoval, M. (2004) Pero ¿quién es Chimamanda? *El País*. [Online]. [Accessed 19 April 2018].

Available from: <http://cultura.elpais.com/cultura/2014/03/18/actualidad/1395173061_371389.html>

RECOMMENDED READING

- Achebe, C. (2013) *There Was a Country: A Personal History of Biafra*. London: Penguin.
- Said, E. W. (2003) *Orientalism*. London: Penguin.

ADAPTATION

- *Half of a Yellow Sun*. (2013) [Film]. Biyi Bandele. Dir. Nigeria: Shareman Media/Slate Films.

www.brightsummaries.com

Ebook EAN: 9782808002240

Paperback EAN: 9782808002257

Legal Deposit: D/2017/12603/633

Cover: © Primento

Digital conception by Primento, the digital partner of publishers.

Printed in Great Britain
by Amazon

51068509R00037